First published in the United States, Great Britain, Canada,
Australia, and New Zealand in 1988 by North-South Books,
an imprint of Nord-Süd Verlag AG, Gossau Zürich, Switzerland.
Reissued in a larger format in paperback in 1996.

Distributed in the United States by North-South Books Inc., New York.

Library of Congress Cataloging-in-Publication Data
Velthuijs, Max
A birthday cake for Little Bear / Max Velthuijs.
Summary: Little Pig bakes a birthday cake for Little Bear
and all of their friends show up for a taste.
Includes recipe for chocolate cake.
1. Birthdays. 2. Cakes. I. Title
PZ7.V5 LI   1985   87-73270

British Library Cataloguing in Publication Data
Velthuijs, Max
A birthday cake for little bear.
I. Title   II. Eine Geburtstagstorte fur den
kleinen Baren. *English*
833.'914 PZ7

ISBN 1-55858-512-5
Printed in Belgium

Max Velthuijs

A Birthday Cake
for Little Bear

Translated by Rosemary Lanning

North-South Books / New York / London

For all children who like chocolate cake

"It's Little Bear's birthday today," said Little Pig.
"I'll bake him a birthday cake."

He put on his apron and went into the kitchen.

Little Pig set out all the ingredients: butter, sugar, eggs, milk, flour, and baking powder—and he didn't forget the cocoa powder and vanilla extract.

Then he took a bowl, put in the butter and sugar, and beat them well. He added three eggs and the vanilla extract, and stirred again. Finally he folded in the flour, baking powder, and cocoa along with the milk, and stirred the mixture until it was quite smooth.

Little Pig greased a cake pan with butter, dusted it with a little flour, and poured in the cake mixture. Then he put it in the oven.

With a happy sigh Little Pig sat down by the stove to wait. Soon a delicious smell came wafting out. When the cake was done, Little Pig took it carefully out of the oven. Then he removed the cake from the pan and left it to cool.

"I could decorate the cake with strawberries," thought
Little Pig. He ran into the garden and picked a basketful.

Little Pig put the strawberries on the cake, one right in the middle and the rest around the edge.

He carefully piped whipped cream around the cake.
Then Rabbit came along.

"Hey!" said Rabbit. "That smells good! A cake, is it?"

"Yes, but it's not for you," said Little Pig hurriedly.
"It's Little Bear's birthday today."

"I see. Well, it looks lovely, that cake," said Rabbit,
"but does it taste good, I wonder?"

"Of course it does! Why?"

"If you're going to give someone a present, you have
to be sure it's good. Shall I test it for you?"

And Rabbit was already sticking his paw into the cream.

"So?" said Little Pig impatiently.

"I'm not sure," said Rabbit thoughtfully. "I need another taste."

"Let me try it," said Little Pig. He carefully took a tiny bit. "Mmmm, it does taste good."

"I think it ought to be a little sweeter," said Rabbit. Little Pig put another spoonful of sugar into the rest of the cream.

Then Duck came along. "Hello, what's this that looks
so nice?" she quacked cheerfully.

"It's a birthday cake for Little Bear," said Little Pig.
"I'm just going to put a bit more cream on it, and then
you can have a taste."

Duck didn't wait to be asked twice. "Fantastic!" she
said with her beak full. "Just right. Not too sweet."
Then Rabbit and Little Pig had to have another taste.
"Duck's right," said Rabbit. "Now it tastes perfect."

"But we haven't tasted the actual cake!" exclaimed Duck. So they all took a slice. It tasted wonderful. They all took another slice right away, so they could be sure that the cake really was all right.

Suddenly Little Bear appeared. "That looks good," he growled with a smile. "What is it? Can I have a bit too?"

"Of course," said Little Pig. "It's your birthday, after all, and the cake is for you."

"For me!" said Little Bear. "A real birthday cake, for me?" He beamed with pleasure as he bit into a big slice. "This is good! I've never tasted anything so delicious."

"The cake looked even prettier," said Little Pig, "when it had strawberries and whipped cream on it. But you see, we had to try it to see how it tasted."

"How did it taste?"

"Wonderful! Scrumptious!" exclaimed all three.

"Come on, let's enjoy the rest of the cake in the garden,"
said Duck.

"And Little Bear can have the piece with the strawberry
and the little bit of cream left on it," said Little Pig.

Then they all sat down together at the back of the house and ate the rest of the cake, down to the last crumb. And because Little Bear's birthday came only once a year, they played, chatted, and sang songs for the whole afternoon.

It wasn't until sunset that Little Bear said good-bye to his friends.

"A birthday cake decorated with strawberries and cream," said Little Bear happily to himself, over and over, on his way home.

"This was the best birthday I've ever had."

Recipe for Little Bear's Birthday Cake

BRITISH MEASURES	AMERICAN MEASURES
6 oz (170g) butter	¾ cup (1½ sticks) butter
6 oz (170g) caster sugar	¾ cup granulated sugar
3 eggs (size 3)	3 large eggs
5 oz (140g) plain flour	1¼ cup all-purpose flour
2 level tsps baking powder	2 level tsps baking powder
3 tbsps cocoa powder	3 tbsps cocoa powder
1 tsp vanilla extract	1 tsp vanilla extract
2-3 tbsps milk	2-3 tbsps milk

Grease and lightly flour an 8" (20 cm) diameter, deep cake pan. Preheat the oven to 350° F (180° C/Circotherm 160° C/Gas Mark 5). Sift together the flour, baking powder, and cocoa. Beat the butter with the sugar until light and fluffy. Whisk the eggs lightly with the vanilla extract and gradually add them to the butter and sugar, beating well after each addition. (Adding a little of the flour and cocoa mixture along with the last of the egg will help keep the batter from curdling.) Gently fold in half the flour and cocoa mixture, then fold in the remainder, together with enough milk to produce a soft mixture that drops easily from your spoon. Spoon the mixture into the pan, level the surface, and bake for 55 minutes to 1 hour, until a toothpick inserted in the middle comes out clean. Cool for 5 minutes before removing the cake from the pan. When the cake is completely cool, it can be decorated with fudge icing or, for a really special occasion, strawberries and whipped cream.